Cookies

"What are you doing?"
Little Bear asked Big Bear.

"I am making cookie mix,"
Big Bear replied.

"May I lick the bowl?"
Little Bear asked.

"When I have finished,"
said Big Bear.

The cookie mix was made
but the oven was not ready.
Big Bear went outside
to wait for the oven.

Little Bear came in.

He saw the bowl of cookie mix.

"Big Bear has gone," he said.

"He must be finished."

When Big Bear came back,
he cried, "Oh! Little Bear!
Why are you eating
my cookie mix?"

"I thought you had finished,"
Little Bear replied.
"I thought you left this
in the bowl for me."

Big Bear and Little Bear
ate the rest of the cookie mix.
Big Bear said, "It is better
when it is not cooked."